A CHRISTMAS MEMORY

TRUMAN CAPOTE

A Christmas Memory

ONE CHRISTMAS

THE THANKSGIVING VISITOR

THE MODERN LIBRARY

NEW YORK

29

TRUMAN CAPOTE

TRUMAN CAPOTE was born Truman Streckfus Persons on September 30, 1924, in New Orleans. His early years were affected by an unsettled family life. He was turned over to the care of his mother's family in Monroeville, Alabama; his father was imprisoned for fraud; his parents divorced and then fought a bitter custody battle over Truman. Eventually he moved to New York City to live with his mother and her second husband, a Cuban businessman whose name he adopted. The young Capote got a job as a copyboy at *The New Yorker* in the early forties, but was fired for inadvertently offending Robert Frost. The publication of his early stories in *Harper's Bazaar* established his literary reputation when he was in his twenties, and his novels *Other Voices, Other Rooms* (1948), a gothic coming-of-age story that Capote described as "an attempt to exorcise demons," and *The Grass Harp* (1951), a gentler fantasy rooted in his Alabama years, consolidated his precocious fame.

From the start of his career Capote associated himself with a wide range of writers and artists, high-society figures, and international celebrities, gaining frequent media attention for his exuberant social life. He collected his stories in *A Tree of Night* (1949) and published the novella *Breakfast at Tiffany's* (1958), but devoted his energies increasingly to the stage—adapting *The Grass Harp* into a play and writing the musical *House of Flowers* (1954)—and to journalism, of which the earliest examples were *Local Color* (1950) and *The Muses Are Heard* (1956). He made a brief foray into the movies to write the screenplay for John Huston's *Beat the Devil* (1954).

Capote's interest in the murder of a family in Kansas led to the prolonged investigation that provided the basis for *In Cold Blood* (1966), his most successful and acclaimed book. By "treating a real event with fictional techniques," Capote intended to create a new synthesis: something both "immaculately factual" and a work of art. However its genre was defined, from the moment it began to appear in serialized form in *The New Yorker* the book exerted a fascination among a wider readership than Capote's writing had ever attracted before. The abundantly publicized masked ball at the Plaza Hotel with which he celebrated the completion of *In Cold Blood* was an iconic event of the 1960s, and for a time Capote was a constant presence on television and in magazines, even trying his hand at movie acting in *Murder by Death.*

He worked for many years on *Answered Prayers,* an ultimately unfinished novel that was intended to be the distillation of everything he had observed in his life among the rich and famous; an excerpt from it published in *Esquire* in 1975 appalled many of Capote's wealthy friends for its revelation of intimate secrets, and he found himself excluded from the world he had once dominated. In his later years he published two collections of fiction and essays, *The Dogs Bark* (1973) and *Music for Chameleons* (1980). He died on August 25, 1984, after years of problems with drugs and alcohol.

The Complete Stories of Truman Capote and *Too Brief a Treat: The Letters of Truman Capote* were published in 2004. In 2005, *Summer Crossing,* his first novel long believed to be lost, was published around the world.

Contents

A Christmas Memory

*I*magine a morning in late November. A coming of winter morning more than twenty years ago. Consider the kitchen of a spreading old house in a country town. A great black stove is its main feature; but there is also a big round table and a fireplace with two rocking chairs placed in front of it. Just today the fireplace commenced its seasonal roar.

A woman with shorn white hair is standing at the kitchen window. She is wearing tennis shoes and a shapeless gray sweater over a summery calico dress. She is small and sprightly, like a bantam hen; but, due to a long youthful illness, her shoulders are pitifully hunched. Her face is remarkable—not unlike Lincoln's, craggy like that, and tinted by sun and wind; but it is delicate too, finely boned, and her eyes are sherry-colored and timid. "Oh my," she exclaims, her breath smoking the windowpane, "it's fruitcake weather!"

The person to whom she is speaking is myself. I am seven; she is sixty-something. We are cousins, very distant ones, and we have lived together—well, as long as I can remember. Other people inhabit the house, relatives; and though they have power over us, and frequently make us cry, we are not, on the whole, too much aware of them. We are each other's best friend. She calls me Buddy, in memory of a boy who was formerly her best friend. The other Buddy died in the 1880's, when she was still a child. She is still a child.

"I knew it before I got out of bed," she says, turning away from the window with a purposeful excitement in her eyes. "The courthouse bell sounded so cold and clear. And there were no birds singing; they've gone to warmer country, yes indeed. Oh, Buddy, stop stuffing biscuit and fetch our buggy. Help me find my hat. We've thirty cakes to bake."

It's always the same: a morning arrives in November, and my friend, as though officially inaugurating the Christmas time of year that exhilarates her imagination and fuels the blaze of her heart, announces: "It's fruitcake weather! Fetch our buggy. Help me find my hat."

The hat is found, a straw cartwheel corsaged with velvet roses out-of-doors has faded: it once belonged to a more fashionable relative. Together, we guide our buggy, a dilapidated baby carriage, out to the garden and into a grove of pecan trees. The buggy is mine; that is, it was bought for me when I was born. It is made of wicker, rather unraveled, and the wheels wobble like a drunkard's legs. But it is a faithful object; springtimes, we take it to the woods and fill it with flowers, herbs, wild fern for our porch pots; in the summer, we pile it with picnic paraphernalia and sugar-cane fishing poles and roll it down to the edge of a creek; it has its winter uses, too: as a truck for hauling firewood from the yard to the kitchen, as a warm bed for Queenie, our tough little orange and white rat terrier who has survived distemper and two rattlesnake bites. Queenie is trotting beside it now.

Three hours later we are back in the kitchen hulling a heaping buggyload of windfall pecans. Our backs hurt from gathering them: how hard they were to find (the main crop having been shaken off the trees and sold by the orchard's owners, who are not us) among the concealing leaves, the frosted, deceiving grass. Caarackle! A cheery crunch, scraps of miniature thunder sound as the shells collapse and the golden mound of sweet oily ivory meat mounts in the milk-glass bowl. Queenie begs to taste, and now and again my friend sneaks her a mite, though insisting we deprive ourselves. "We mustn't, Buddy. If we start, we won't stop. And there's scarcely enough as there is. For thirty cakes." The kitchen is growing dark. Dusk turns the window into a mirror: our reflections mingle with the rising moon as we work by the fireside in the firelight. At last, when the moon is quite high, we toss the final hull into the fire and, with joined sighs, watch it catch flame. The buggy is empty, the bowl is brimful.

We eat our supper (cold biscuits, bacon, blackberry jam) and discuss tomorrow. Tomorrow the kind of work I like best begins: buying. Cherries and citron, ginger and vanilla and canned Hawaiian pineapple, rinds and raisins and walnuts and whiskey and oh, so much flour, butter, so many eggs, spices, flavorings: why, we'll need a pony to pull the buggy home.

But before these purchases can be made, there is the question of money. Neither of us has any. Except for skinflint sums persons in the house occasionally provide (a dime is considered very big money); or what we earn ourselves from various activities: holding rummage sales, selling buckets of hand-picked blackberries, jars of homemade jam and apple jelly and peach preserves, rounding up flowers for funerals and weddings. Once we won seventy-ninth prize, five dollars, in a national football contest. Not that we know a fool thing about football. It's just that we enter any contest we hear about: at the moment our hopes are centered on the fifty-thousand-dollar Grand Prize being offered to name a new brand of coffee (we suggested "A.M."; and, after some hesitation, for my friend thought it perhaps sacrilegious, the slogan "A.M.! Amen!"). To tell the truth, our only *really* profitable enterprise was the Fun and Freak Museum we conducted in a back-yard woodshed two summers ago. The Fun was a stereopticon with slide views of Washington and New York lent us by a relative who had been to those places (she was furious when she discovered why we'd borrowed it); the Freak was a three-legged biddy chicken hatched by one of our own hens. Everybody hereabouts wanted to see that biddy: we charged grownups a nickel, kids two cents. And took in a good twenty dollars before the museum shut down due to the decease of the main attraction.

But one way and another we do each year accumulate Christmas savings, a Fruitcake Fund. These moneys we keep hidden in an ancient bead purse under a loose board under the floor under a chamber

pot under my friend's bed. The purse is seldom removed from this safe location except to make a deposit, or, as happens every Saturday, a withdrawal; for
on Saturdays I am allowed ten cents to go to the picture show. My friend has never been to a picture show,
nor does she intend to: "I'd rather hear you tell the
story, Buddy. That way I can imagine it more. Besides,
a person my age shouldn't squander their eyes. When
the Lord comes, let me see him clear." In addition to
never having seen a movie, she has never: eaten in a
restaurant, traveled more than five miles from home,
received or sent a telegram, read anything except
funny papers and the Bible, worn cosmetics, cursed,
wished someone harm, told a lie on purpose, let a hungry dog go hungry. Here are a few things she has done,
does do: killed with a hoe the biggest rattlesnake ever
seen in this county (sixteen rattles), dip snuff (secretly), tame hummingbirds (just try it) till they bal-
ance on her finger, tell ghost stories (we both believe in
ghosts) so tingling they chill you in July, talk to herself,

take walks in the rain, grow the prettiest japonicas in town, know the recipe for every sort of old-time Indian cure, including a magical wart-remover.

Now, with supper finished, we retire to the room in a faraway part of the house where my friend sleeps in a scrap-quilt-covered iron bed painted rose pink, her favorite color. Silently, wallowing in the pleasures of conspiracy, we take the bead purse from its secret place and spill its contents on the scrap quilt. Dollar bills, tightly rolled and green as May buds. Somber fifty-cent pieces, heavy enough to weight a dead man's eyes. Lovely dimes, the liveliest coin, the one that really jingles. Nickels and quarters, worn smooth as creek pebbles. But mostly a hateful heap of bitter-odored pennies. Last summer others in the house contracted to pay us a penny for every twenty-five flies we killed. Oh, the carnage of August: the flies that flew to heaven! Yet it was not work in which we took pride. And, as we sit counting pennies, it is as though we were back tabulating dead flies. Neither of us had a head for figures; we count slowly, lose track, start again. According to her calculations, we have $12.73. According to mine, exactly $13. "I do hope you're wrong, Buddy. We can't mess around with thirteen. The cakes will fall. Or put somebody in the cemetery. Why, I wouldn't dream of getting out of bed on the thirteenth." This is true: she always spends thirteenths in bed. So, to be on the safe side, we subtract a penny and toss it out the window.

Of the ingredients that go into our fruitcakes, whiskey is the most expensive, as well as the hardest to obtain: State laws forbid its sale. But everybody knows you can buy a bottle from Mr. Haha Jones. And the next day, having completed our more prosaic shopping, we set out for Mr. Haha's business address, a "sinful" (to quote public opinion) fish-fry and dancing café down by the river. We've been there before, and on the same errand; but in previous years our dealings have been with Haha's wife, an iodine-dark Indian woman with brassy peroxided hair and a dead-tired disposition. Actually, we've never laid eyes on her husband, though we've heard that he's an Indian too. A giant with razor scars across his cheeks. They call him Haha because he's so gloomy, a man who never laughs. As we approach his café (a large log cabin festooned inside and out with chains of garish-gay naked light bulbs and standing by the river's muddy edge under the shade of river trees where moss drifts through the branches like gray mist) our steps slow down. Even Queenie stops prancing and sticks close by. People have been murdered in Haha's café. Cut to pieces. Hit on the head. There's a case coming up in court next month. Naturally these goings-on happen at night when the colored lights cast crazy patterns and the victrola wails. In the daytime Haha's is shabby and deserted. I knock at the door, Queenie barks, my friend calls: "Mrs. Haha, ma'am? Anyone to home?"

Footsteps. The door opens. Our hearts overturn. It's Mr. Haha Jones himself! And he *is* a giant; he *does* have scars; he *doesn't* smile. No, he glowers at us through Satan-tilted eyes and demands to know: "What you want with Haha?"

For a moment we are too paralyzed to tell. Presently my friend half-finds her voice, a whispery voice at best: "If you please, Mr. Haha, we'd like a quart of your finest whiskey."

His eyes tilt more. Would you believe it? Haha is smiling! Laughing, too. "Which one of you is a drinkin' man?"

"It's for making fruitcakes, Mr. Haha. Cooking."

This sobers him. He frowns. "That's no way to waste good whiskey." Nevertheless, he retreats into the shadowed café and seconds later appears carrying a bottle of daisy yellow unlabeled liquor. He demonstrates its sparkle in the sunlight and says: "Two dollars."

We pay him with nickels and dimes and pennies. Suddenly, jangling the coins in his hand like a fistful of dice, his face softens. "Tell you what," he proposes, pouring the money back into our bead purse, "just send me one of them fruitcakes instead."

"Well," my friend remarks on our way home, "there's a lovely man. We'll put an extra cup of raisins in *his* cake."

The black stove, stoked with coal and firewood, glows like a lighted pumpkin. Eggbeaters whirl, spoons spin round in bowls of butter and sugar, vanilla sweetens the air, ginger spices it; melting, nose-tingling odors saturate the kitchen, suffuse the house, drift out to the world on puffs of chimney smoke. In four days our work is done. Thirty-one cakes, dampened with whiskey, bask on window sills and shelves.

Who are they for?

Friends. Not necessarily neighbor friends: indeed, the larger share are intended for persons we've met maybe once, perhaps not at all. People who've struck our fancy. Like President Roosevelt. Like the Reverend and Mrs. J. C. Lucey, Baptist missionaries to Borneo who lectured here last winter. Or the little knife grinder who comes through town twice a year. Or Abner Packer, the driver of the six o'clock bus from Mobile, who exchanges waves with us every day as he passes in a dust-cloud whoosh. Or the young Wistons, a California couple whose car one afternoon broke down outside the house and who spent a pleasant hour chatting with us on the porch (young Mr. Wiston snapped our picture, the only one we've ever had taken). Is it because my friend is shy with everyone *except* strangers that these strangers, and merest acquaintances, seem to us our truest friends? I think yes. Also, the scrapbooks we keep of thank-you's on White House stationery, time-to-time communications from California and Borneo, the knife grinder's penny post cards, make us feel connected to eventful worlds beyond the kitchen with its view of a sky that stops.

Now a nude December fig branch grates against the window. The kitchen is empty, the cakes are gone; yesterday we carted the last of them to the post office, where the cost of stamps turned our purse inside out. We're broke. That rather depresses me, but my friend insists on celebrating—with two inches of whiskey left in Haha's bottle. Queenie has a spoonful in a bowl of coffee (she likes her coffee chicory-flavored and strong). The rest we divide between a pair of jelly glasses. We're both quite awed at the prospect of drinking straight whiskey; the taste of it brings screwed-up expressions and sour shudders. But by and by we begin to sing, the two of us singing different songs simultaneously. I don't know the words to mine, just: *Come on along, come on along, to the dark-town strutters' ball.* But I can dance: that's what I mean to be, a tap dancer in the movies. My dancing shadow rollicks on the walls; our voices rock the chinaware; we giggle: as if unseen hands were tickling us. Queenie rolls on her back, her paws plow the air, something like a grin stretches her black lips. Inside myself, I feel warm and sparky as those crumbling logs, carefree as the wind in the chimney. My friend waltzes round the stove, the hem of her poor calico skirt pinched between her fingers as though it were a party dress: *Show me the way to go home,* she sings, her tennis shoes squeaking on the floor. *Show me the way to go home.*

Enter: two relatives. Very angry. Potent with eyes that scold, tongues that scald. Listen to what they have to say, the words tumbling together into a wrathful tune: "A child of seven! whiskey on his breath! are you out of your mind? feeding a child of seven! must be loony! road to ruination! remember Cousin Kate? Uncle Charlie? Uncle Charlie's brother-in-law? shame! scandal! humiliation! kneel, pray, beg the Lord!"

Queenie sneaks under the stove. My friend gazes at her shoes, her chin quivers, she lifts her skirt and blows her nose and runs to her room. Long after the town has gone to sleep and the house is silent except for the chimings of clocks and the sputter of fading fires, she is weeping into a pillow already as wet as a widow's handkerchief.

"Don't cry," I say, sitting at the bottom of her bed and shivering despite my flannel nightgown that smells of last winter's cough syrup, "don't cry," I beg, teasing her toes, tickling her feet, "you're too old for that."

"It's because," she hiccups, "I *am* too old. Old and funny."

"Not funny. Fun. More fun than anybody. Listen.

If you don't stop crying you'll be so tired tomorrow we can't go cut a tree."

She straightens up. Queenie jumps on the bed (where Queenie is not allowed) to lick her cheeks. "I know where we'll find real pretty trees, Buddy. And holly, too. With berries big as your eyes. It's way off in the woods. Farther than we've ever been. Papa used to bring us Christmas trees from there: carry them on his shoulder. That's fifty years ago. Well, now: I can't wait for morning."

Morning. Frozen rime lusters the grass; the sun, round as an orange and orange as hot-weather moons, balances on the horizon, burnishes the silvered winter woods. A wild turkey calls. A renegade hog grunts in the undergrowth. Soon, by the edge of knee-deep, rapid-running water, we have to abandon the buggy. Queenie wades the stream first, paddles across barking complaints at the swiftness of the current, the pneumonia-making coldness of it. We follow, holding our shoes and equipment (a hatchet, a burlap sack) above our heads. A mile more: of chastising thorns, burs and briers that catch at our clothes; of rusty pine needles brilliant with gaudy fungus and molted feathers. Here, there, a flash, a flutter, an ecstasy of shrillings remind us that not all the birds have flown south. Always, the path unwinds through lemony sun pools and pitch vine tunnels. Another creek to cross: a disturbed armada of speckled trout froths the water round us, and frogs the size of plates practice belly flops; beaver workmen are building a dam. On the farther shore, Queenie shakes herself and trembles. My friend shivers, too: not with cold but enthusiasm. One of her hat's ragged roses sheds a petal as she lifts her head and inhales the pine-heavy air. "We're almost there, can you smell it, Buddy?" she says, as though we were approaching an ocean.

And, indeed, it is a kind of ocean. Scented acres of holiday trees, prickly-leafed holly. Red berries shiny as Chinese bells: black crows swoop upon them screaming. Having stuffed our burlap sacks with enough greenery and crimson to garland a dozen windows, we set about choosing a tree. "It should be," muses my friend, "twice as tall as a boy. So a boy can't steal the star." The one we pick is twice as tall as me. A brave handsome brute that survives thirty hatchet strokes before it keels with a creaking rending cry. Lugging it like a kill, we commence the long trek out. Every few yards we abandon the struggle, sit down and pant. But we have the strength of triumphant huntsmen; that and the tree's virile, icy perfume revive us, goad us on. Many compliments accompany our sunset return along the red clay road to town; but my friend is sly and noncommittal when passers-by praise the treasure perched in our buggy: what a fine tree and where did it come from? "Yonderways," she murmurs vaguely. Once a car stops and the rich mill owner's lazy wife leans out and whines: "Giveya twobits cash for that ol tree." Ordinarily my friend is afraid of saying no; but on this occasion she promptly shakes her head: "We wouldn't take a dollar." The mill owner's wife persists. "A dollar, my foot! Fifty cents. That's my last offer. Goodness, woman, you can get another one." In answer, my friend gently reflects: "I doubt it. There's never two of anything."

Home: Queenie slumps by the fire and sleeps till tomorrow, snoring loud as a human.

A trunk in the attic contains: a shoebox of ermine tails (off the opera cape of a curious lady who once rented a room in the house), coils of frazzled tinsel gone gold with age, one silver star, a brief rope of dilapidated, undoubtedly dangerous candy-like light bulbs. Excellent decorations, as far as they go, which isn't far enough: my friend wants our tree to blaze "like a Baptist window," droop with weighty snows of ornament. But we can't afford the made-in-Japan splendors at the five-and-dime. So we do what we've always done: sit for days at the kitchen table with scissors and crayons and stacks of colored paper. I make sketches and my friend cuts them out: lots of cats, fish too (because they're easy to draw), some apples, some watermelons, a few winged angels devised from saved-up sheets of Hershey-bar tin foil. We use safety pins to attach these creations to the tree; as a final touch, we sprinkle the branches with shredded cotton (picked in August for this purpose). My friend, surveying the effect, clasps her hands together. "Now honest, Buddy. Doesn't it look good enough to eat?" Queenie tries to eat an angel.

After weaving and ribboning holly wreaths for all the front windows, our next project is the fashioning of family gifts. Tie-dye scarves for the ladies, for the men a home-brewed lemon and licorice and aspirin syrup to be taken "at the first Symptoms of a Cold and after Hunting." But when it comes time for making each other's gift, my friend and I separate to work secretly. I would like to buy her a pearl-handled knife, a radio, a whole pound of chocolate-covered cherries (we tasted some once and she always swears: "I could live on them, Buddy, Lord yes I could—and that's not taking His name in vain"). Instead, I am building her a kite. She would like to give me a bicycle (she's said so on several million occasions: "If only I could, Buddy. It's bad enough in life to do without something *you* want; but confound it, what gets my goat is not being able to give somebody something you want *them* to have. Only one of these days I will, Buddy. Locate you a bike. Don't ask how. Steal it, maybe"). Instead, I'm fairly certain that she is building me a kite—the same as last year, and the year before: the year before that we exchanged slingshots. All of which is fine by me. For we are champion kite-flyers who study the wind like sailors; my friend, more accomplished than I, can get a kite aloft when there isn't enough breeze to carry clouds.

Christmas Eve afternoon we scrape together a nickel and go to the butcher's to buy Queenie's traditional gift, a good gnawable beef bone. The bone, wrapped in funny paper, is placed high in the tree near the silver star. Queenie knows it's there. She squats at the foot of the tree staring up in a trance of greed: when bedtime arrives she refuses to budge. Her excitement is equaled by my own. I kick the covers and turn my pillow as though it were a scorching summer's night. Somewhere a rooster crows: falsely, for the sun is still on the other side of the world.

"Buddy, are you awake?" It is my friend, calling from her room, which is next to mine; and an instant later she is sitting on my bed holding a candle. "Well, I can't sleep a hoot," she declares. "My mind's jumping like a jack rabbit. Buddy, do you think Mrs. Roosevelt will serve our cake at dinner?" We huddle in the bed, and she squeezes my hand I-love-you. "Seems like your hand used to be so much smaller. I guess I hate to see you grow up. When you're grown up, will we still be friends?" I say always. "But I feel so bad, Buddy. I wanted so bad to give you a bike. I tried to sell my cameo Papa gave me. Buddy—" she hesitates, as though embarrassed—"I made you another kite." Then I confess that I made her one, too; and we laugh. The candle burns too short to hold. Out it goes, exposing the starlight, the stars spinning at the window like a visible caroling that slowly, slowly daybreak silences. Possibly we doze; but the beginnings of dawn splash us like cold water: we're up, wide-eyed and wandering while we wait for others to waken. Quite deliberately my friend drops a kettle on the kitchen floor. I tap-dance in front of closed doors. One by one the household emerges, looking as though they'd like to kill us both; but its Christmas, so they can't. First, a gorgeous breakfast: just everything you can imagine—from flapjacks and fried squirrel to hominy grits and honey-in-the-comb. Which puts everyone in a good humor except my friend and I. Frankly, we're so impatient to get at the presents we can't eat a mouthful.

Well, I'm disappointed. Who wouldn't be? With socks, a Sunday school shirt, some handkerchiefs, a hand-me-down sweater and a year's subscription to a religious magazine for children. *The Little Shepherd*. It makes me boil. It really does.

My friend has a better haul. A sack of Satsumas, that's her best present. She is proudest, however, of a white wool shawl knitted by her married sister. But she *says* her favorite gift is the kite I built her. And it *is* very beautiful, though not as beautiful as the one she made me, which is blue and scattered with gold and green Good Conduct stars; moreover, my name is painted on it, "Buddy."

"Buddy, the wind is blowing."

The wind is blowing, and nothing will do till we've run to a pasture below the house where Queenie has scooted to bury her bone (and where, a winter hence, Queenie will be buried, too). There, plunging through the healthy waist-high grass, we unreel our kites, feel them twitching at the string like sky fish as they swim into the wind. Satisfied, sun-warmed, we sprawl in the grass and peel Satsumas and watch our kites cavort. Soon I forget the socks and hand-me-down sweater. I'm as happy as if we'd already won the fifty-thousand-dollar Grand Prize in that coffee-naming contest.

"My, how foolish I am!" my friend cries, suddenly alert, like a woman remembering too late she has biscuits in the oven. "You know what I've always thought?" she asks in a tone of discovery, and not smiling at me but a point beyond. "I've always thought a body would have to be sick and dying before they saw the Lord.

And I imagined that when He came it would be like looking at the Baptist window: pretty as colored glass with the sun pouring through, such a shine you don't know it's getting dark. And it's been a comfort: to think of that shine taking away all the spooky feeling. But I'll wager it never happens. I'll wager at the very end a body realizes the Lord has already shown Himself. That things as they are"—her hand circles in a gesture that gathers clouds and kites and grass and Queenie pawing earth over her bone—"just what they've always seen, was seeing Him. As for me, I could leave the world with today in my eyes."

*T*his is our last Christmas together.

Life separates us. Those who Know Best decide that I belong in a military school. And so follows a miserable succession of bugle-blowing prisons, grim reveille-ridden summer camps. I have a new home too. But it doesn't count. Home is where my friend is, and there I never go.

And there she remains, puttering around the kitchen. Alone with Queenie. Then alone. ("Buddy dear," she writes in her wild hard-to-read script, "yesterday Jim Macy's horse kicked Queenie bad. Be thankful she didn't feel much. I wrapped her in a Fine Linen sheet and rode her in the buggy down to Simpson's pasture where she can be with all her Bones . . ."). For a few Novembers she continues to bake her fruitcakes single-handed; not as many, but some: and, of course, she always sends me "the best of the batch." Also, in every letter she encloses a dime wadded in toilet paper: "See a picture show and write me the story." But gradually in her letters she tends to confuse me with her other friend, the Buddy who died in the 1880's; more and more thirteenths are not the only days she stays in bed: a morning arrives in November, a leafless birdless coming of winter morning, when she cannot rouse herself to exclaim: "Oh my, it's fruitcake weather!"

And when that happens, I know it. A message saying so merely confirms a piece of news some secret vein had already received, severing from me an irreplaceable part of myself, letting it loose like a kite on a broken string. That is why, walking across a school campus on this particular December morning, I keep searching the sky. As if I expected to see, rather like hearts, a lost pair of kites hurrying toward heaven.

One Christmas

for Gloria Dunphy

*F*irst, a brief autobiographical prologue. My mother, who was exceptionally intelligent, was the most beautiful girl in Alabama. Everyone said so, and it was true; and when she was sixteen she married a twenty-eight-year-old businessman who came from a good New Orleans family. The marriage lasted a year. My mother was too young to be a mother or a wife; she was also too ambitious—she wanted to go to college and to have a career. So she left her husband; and as for what to do with me, she deposited me in the care of her large Alabama family.

Over the years, I seldom saw either of my parents. My father was occupied in New Orleans, and my mother, after graduating from college, was making a success for herself in New York. So far as I was concerned, this was not an unpleasant situation. I was happy where I was. I had many kindly relatives, aunts and uncles and cousins, particularly *one* cousin, an elderly, white-haired, slightly crippled woman named Sook. Miss Sook Faulk. I had other friends, but she was by far my best friend.

It was Sook who told me about Santa Claus, his flowing beard, his red suit, his jangling present-filled sled, and I believed her, just as I believed that everything was God's will, or the Lord's, as Sook always called Him. If I stubbed my toe, or fell off a horse, or caught a good-sized fish at the creek—well, good or bad, it was all the Lord's will. And that was what Sook said when she received the frightening news from New Orleans: My father wanted me to travel there to spend Christmas with him.

I cried. I didn't want to go. I'd never left this small,

isolated Alabama town surrounded by forests and farms and rivers. I'd never gone to sleep without Sook combing her fingers through my hair and kissing me good-night. Then, too, I was afraid of strangers, and my father was a stranger. I had seen him several times, but the memory was a haze; I had no idea what he was like. But, as Sook said: "It's the Lord's will. And who knows, Buddy, maybe you'll see snow."

Snow! Until I could read myself, Sook read me many stories, and it seemed a lot of snow was in almost all of them. Drifting, dazzling fairytale flakes. It was something I dreamed about; something magical and mysterious that I wanted to see and feel and touch. Of course I never had, and neither had Sook; how could we, living in a hot place like Alabama? I don't know why she thought I would see snow in New Orleans, for New Orleans is even hotter. Never mind. She was just trying to give me courage to make the trip.

I had a new suit. It had a card pinned to the lapel with my name and address. That was in case I got lost. You see, I had to make the trip alone. By bus. Well, everybody thought I'd be safe with my tag. Everybody but me. I was scared to death; and angry. Furious at my father, this stranger, who was forcing me to leave home and be away from Sook at Christmastime.

It was a four-hundred-mile trip, something like that. My first stop was in Mobile. I changed buses there, and rode along forever and forever through swampy lands and along seacoasts until we arrived in a loud city tinkling with trolley cars and packed with dangerous foreign-looking people.

That was New Orleans.

And suddenly, as I stepped off the bus, a man swept me in his arms, squeezed the breath out of me; he was laughing, he was crying—a tall, good-looking man, laughing and crying. He said: "Don't you know me? Don't you know your daddy?"

I was speechless. I didn't say a word until at last, while we were riding along in a taxi, I asked: "Where is it?"

"Our house? It's not far—"

"Not the house. The snow."

"What snow?"

"I thought there would be a lot of snow."

He looked at me strangely, but laughed. "There never has been any snow in New Orleans. Not that I heard of. But listen. Hear that thunder? It's sure going to rain!"

I don't know what scared me most, the thunder, the sizzling zigzags of lightning that followed it—or my father. That night, when I went to bed, it was still raining. I said my prayers and prayed that I would soon be home with Sook. I didn't know how I could ever go to sleep without Sook to kiss me good-night. The fact was, I couldn't go to sleep, so I began to wonder what Santa Claus would bring me. I wanted a pearl-handled knife. And a big set of jigsaw puzzles. A cowboy hat with matching lasso. And a B.B. rifle to shoot sparrows. (Years later, when I did have a B.B. gun, I shot a mockingbird and a bobwhite, and I can never forget the regret I felt, the grief; I never killed another thing, and every fish I caught I threw back into the water.) And I wanted a box of crayons. And, most of all, a radio but I knew that was impossible: I didn't know ten people who had radios. Remember, this was the Depression, and in the Deep South houses furnished with radios or refrigerators were rare.

My father had both. He seemed to have everything—a car with a rumble seat, not to mention an old, pink pretty little house in the French Quarter with iron-lace balconies and a secret patio garden colored with flowers and cooled by a fountain shaped like a mermaid. He also had a half-dozen, I'd say full-dozen, lady friends. Like my mother, my father had not remarried; but they both had determined admirers and, willingly or not, eventually walked the path to the altar—in fact, my father walked it six times.

So you can see he must have had charm; and, indeed, he seemed to charm most people—everybody except me. That was because he embarrassed me so, always hauling me around to meet his friends, everybody from his banker to the barber who shaved him every day. And, of course, all his lady friends. And the worst part: All the time he was hugging and kissing me and bragging about me. I felt so ashamed. First of all, there was nothing to brag about. I was a real country boy. I believed in Jesus, and faithfully said my prayers. I knew Santa Claus existed. And at home in Alabama, except to go to church, I never wore shoes; winter or summer.

It was pure torture, being pulled along the streets of New Orleans in those tightly laced, hot as hell, heavy as lead shoes. I don't know what was worse—the shoes or the food. Back home I was used to fried chicken and collard greens and butter beans and corn bread and other comforting things. But these New Orleans restaurants! I will never forget my first oyster, it was like a bad dream sliding down my throat; decades passed before I swallowed another. As for all that spicy Creole cookery—just to think of it gave me heartburn. No sir, I hankered after biscuits right from the stove and milk fresh from the cows and homemade molasses straight from the bucket.

My poor father had no idea how miserable I was, partly because I never let him see it, certainly never told him; and partly because, despite my mother's protest, he had managed to get legal custody of me for this Christmas holiday.

He would say: "Tell the truth. Don't you want to come and live here with me in New Orleans?"

"I can't."

"What do you mean you can't?"

"I miss Sook. I miss Queenie; we have a little rat terrier, a funny little thing. But we both love her."

He said: "Don't you love me?"

I said: "Yes." But the truth was, except for Sook and Queenie and a few cousins and a picture of my beautiful mother beside my bed, I had no real idea of what love meant.

I soon found out. The day before Christmas, as we were walking along Canal Street, I stopped dead still, mesmerized by a magical object that I saw in the window of a big toy store. It was a model airplane large enough to sit in and pedal like a bicycle. It was green and had a red propeller. I was convinced that if you pedaled fast enough it would take off and fly! Now wouldn't that be something! I could just see my cousins standing on the ground while I flew about among the clouds. Talk about green! I laughed; and laughed and laughed. It was the first thing I'd done that made my father look confident, even though he didn't know what I thought was so funny.

That night I prayed that Santa Claus would bring me the airplane.

My father had already bought a Christmas tree, and we spent a great deal of time at the five 'n' dime picking out things to decorate it with. Then I made a mistake. I put a picture of my mother under the tree. The moment my father saw it he turned white and began to tremble. I didn't know what to do. But he did. He went to a cabinet and took out a tall glass and a bottle. I recognized the bottle because all my Alabama uncles had plenty just like it. Prohibition moonshine. He filled the tall glass and drank it with hardly a pause. After that, it was as though the picture had vanished.

And so I awaited Christmas Eve, and the always exciting advent of fat Santa. Of course, I had never seen a weighted, jangling, belly-swollen giant flop down a chimney and gaily dispense his largesse under a Christmas tree. My cousin Billy Bob, who was a mean little runt but had a brain like a fist made of iron, said it was a lot of hooey, there was no such creature.

"My foot!" he said. "Anybody would believe there was any Santa Claus would believe a mule was a horse." This quarrel took place in the tiny courthouse square. I said: *"There is a Santa Claus because what he does is the Lord's will and whatever is the Lord's will is the truth."* And Billy Bob, spitting on the ground, walked away: "Well, looks like we've got another preacher on our hands."

I always swore I'd never go to sleep on Christmas Eve, I wanted to hear the prancing dance of reindeer on the roof, and to be right there at the foot of the chimney to shake hands with Santa Claus. And on this particular Christmas Eve, nothing, it seemed to me, could be easier than staying awake.

My father's house had three floors and seven

rooms, several of them huge, especially the three leading to the patio garden: a parlor, a dining room and a
"musical" room for those who liked to dance and play
and deal cards. The two floors above were trimmed
with lacy balconies whose dark green iron intricacies
were delicately entwined with bougainvillea and rip-
pling vines of scarlet spider orchids—a plant that re-
sembles lizards flicking their red tongues. It was the
kind of house best displayed by lacquered floors and
some wicker here, some velvet there. It could have
been mistaken for the house of a rich man; rather, it
was the place of a man with an appetite for elegance.
To a poor (but happy) barefoot boy from Alabama it
was a mystery how he managed to satisfy that desire.

But it was no mystery to my mother, who, having
graduated from college, was putting her magnolia de-
lights to full use while struggling to find in New York a
truly suitable fiancé who could afford Sutton Place
apartments and sable coats. No, my father's resources
were familiar to her, though she never mentioned the

matter until many years later, long after she had acquired ropes of pearls to glisten around her sable-wrapped throat.

She had come to visit me in a snobbish New England boarding school (where my tuition was paid by her rich and generous husband), when something I said tossed her into a rage; she shouted: "So you don't know how he lives so well? Charters yachts and cruises the Greek Islands? His *wives*! Think of the whole long string of them. All widows. All rich. *Very* rich. And all much older than he. Too old for any sane young man to marry. That's why you are his only child. And that's why I'll never have another child—I was too young to have any babies, but he was a beast, he wrecked me, he ruined me—"

Just a gigolo, everywhere I go, people stop and stare . . . Moon, moon over Miami . . . This is my first affair, so please be kind . . . Hey, mister, can you spare a dime? . . . Just a gigolo, everywhere I go, people stop and stare . . .

All the while she talked (and I tried not to listen, because by telling me my birth had destroyed her, *she* was destroying me), these tunes ran through my head, or tunes like them. They helped me not to hear her, and they reminded me of the strange haunting party my father had given in New Orleans that Christmas Eve.

The patio was filled with candles, and so were the three rooms leading off it. Most of the guests were gathered in the parlor, where a subdued fire in the fireplace made the Christmas tree glitter; but many others were dancing in the music room and the patio to music from a wind-up Victrola. After I had been introduced to the guests, and been made much of, I had been sent upstairs; but from the terrace outside my French-shuttered bedroom door, I could watch all the party, see all the couples dancing. I watched my father waltz a graceful lady around the pool that surrounded the mermaid fountain. She *was* graceful, and dressed in a wispy silver dress that shimmered in the candlelight; but she was old—at least ten years older than my father, who was then thirty-five.

I suddenly realized my father was by far the

youngest person at his party. None of the ladies, charming as they were, were any younger than the willowy waltzer in the floating silver dress. It was the same with the men, so many of whom were smoking sweet-smelling Havana cigars; more than half of them were old enough to be my father's father.

Then I saw something that made me blink. My father and his agile partner had danced themselves into a niche shadowed by scarlet spider orchids; and they were embracing, kissing. I was so startled, I was so *irate,* I ran into my bedroom, jumped into bed and pulled the covers over my head. What would my nice-looking young father want with an old woman like that! And why didn't all those people downstairs go home so Santa Claus could come? I lay awake for hours listening to them leave, and when my father said good-bye for the last time, I heard him climb the stairs and open my door to peek at me; but I pretended to be asleep.

Several things occurred that kept me awake the whole night. First, the footfalls, the noise of my father running up and down the stairs, breathing heavily. I had to see what he was up to. So I hid on the balcony among the bougainvillea. From there, I had a complete view of the parlor and the Christmas tree and the fireplace where a fire still palely burned. Moreover, I could see my father. He was crawling around under the tree arranging a pyramid of packages. Wrapped in purple paper, and red and gold and white and blue, they rustled as he moved them about. I felt dizzy, for what I saw forced me to reconsider everything. If these were presents intended for me, then obviously they had not been ordered by the Lord and delivered by Santa Claus; no, they were gifts bought and wrapped by my father. Which meant that my rotten little cousin Billy Bob and other rotten kids like him weren't lying when they taunted me and told me there was no Santa Claus. The worst thought was: Had Sook known the truth, and lied to me? No, Sook would never lie to me. She *believed*. It was just that—well, though she was sixty-something, in some ways she was at least as much of a child as I was.

I watched until my father had finished his chores

and blown out the few candles that still burned. I waited until I was sure he was in bed and sound asleep. Then I crept downstairs to the parlor, which still reeked of gardenias and Havana cigars.

I sat there, thinking: Now I will have to be the one to tell Sook the truth. An anger, a weird malice was spiraling inside me: It was not directed towards my father, though he turned out to be its victim.

When the dawn came, I examined the tags attached to each of the packages. They all said: "For Buddy." All but one, which said: "For Evangeline." Evangeline was an elderly colored woman who drank Coca-Cola all day long and weighed three hundred pounds; she was my father's housekeeper—she also mothered him. I decided to open the packages: It was Christmas morning, I was awake, so why not? I won't bother to describe what was inside them: just shirts and sweaters and dull stuff like that. The only thing I appreciated was a quite snazzy cap-pistol. Somehow I got the idea it would be fun to waken my father by firing it. So I did. *Bang. Bang. Bang.*

He raced out of his room, wild-eyed.

Bang. Bang. Bang.

"Buddy—what the hell do you think you're doing?"

Bang. Bang. Bang.

"Stop that!"

I laughed. "Look, Daddy. Look at all the wonderful things Santa Claus brought me."

Calm now, he walked into the parlor and hugged me. "You like what Santa Claus brought you?"

I smiled at him. He smiled at me. There was a tender lingering moment, shattered when I said: "Yes. But what are *you* going to give me, Daddy?" His smile evaporated. His eyes narrowed suspiciously—you could see that he thought I was pulling some kind of stunt. But then he blushed, as though he was ashamed to be thinking what he was thinking. He patted my head, and coughed and said: "Well, I thought I'd wait and let you pick out something you wanted. Is there anything particular you want?"

I reminded him of the airplane we had seen in the toy store on Canal Street. His face sagged. Oh, yes, he remembered the airplane and how expensive it was. Nevertheless, the next day I was sitting in that airplane dreaming I was zooming toward heaven while my father wrote out a check for a happy salesman. There had been some argument about shipping the plane to Alabama, but I was adamant—I insisted it should go with me on the bus that I was taking at two o'clock that afternoon. The salesman settled it by calling the bus company, who said that they could handle the matter easily.

But I wasn't free of New Orleans yet. The problem was a large silver flask of moonshine; maybe it was because of my departure, but anyway my father had been swilling it all day, and on the way to the bus station, he scared me by grabbing my wrist and harshly whispering: "I'm not going to let you go. I can't let you go back to that crazy family in that crazy old house. Just look at what they've done to you. A boy six, almost seven, talking about Santa Claus! It's all their fault, all those sour old spinsters with their Bibles and their knitting needles, those drunken uncles. *Listen* to me, Buddy. There is no God! There *is* no Santa Claus." He was squeezing my wrist so hard that it ached. "Sometimes, oh, God, I think your mother and I, the both of us, we ought to kill ourselves to have let this happen—" (He never killed himself, but my mother did: She walked down the Seconal road thirty years ago.) "Kiss me. Please. Please. Kiss me. Tell your daddy that you love him." But I couldn't speak. I was terrified I was going to miss my bus. And I was worried about my plane, which was strapped to the top of the taxi. "Say it: 'I love you.' Say it. Please. Buddy. Say it."

It was lucky for me that our taxi-driver was a good-hearted man. Because if it hadn't been for his help, and the help of some efficient porters and a friendly policeman, I don't know what would have happened when we reached the station. My father was so wobbly he could hardly walk, but the policeman talked to him, quieted him down, helped him to stand straight, and the taxi-man promised to take him safely home. But my father would not leave until he had seen the porters put me on the bus.

Once I was on the bus, I crouched in a seat and shut my eyes. I felt the strangest pain. A crushing pain that hurt everywhere. I thought if I took off my heavy city shoes, those crucifying monsters, the agony would ease. I took them off, but the mysterious pain did not leave me. In a way it never has; never will.

Twelve hours later I was home in bed. The room was dark. Sook was sitting beside me, rocking in a rocking chair, a sound as soothing as ocean waves. I had tried to tell her everything that had happened, and only stopped when I was hoarse as a howling dog. She stroked her fingers through my hair, and said: "Of course there is a Santa Claus. It's just that no single somebody could do all he has to do. So the Lord has spread the task among us all. That's why everybody is Santa Claus. I am. You are. Even your cousin Billy Bob. Now go to sleep. Count stars. Think of the quietest thing. Like snow. I'm sorry you didn't get to see any. But now snow is falling through the stars—" Stars sparkled, snow whirled inside my head; the last thing I remembered was the peaceful voice of the Lord telling me something I must do. And the next day I did it. I went with Sook to the post office and bought a penny postcard. That same postcard exists today. It was found in my father's safety deposit box when he died last year. Here is what I had written him: *Hello pop hope you are well I am and I am lurning to pedel my plain so fast I will soon be in the sky so keep your eyes open and yes I love you Buddy.*

The Thanksgiving
Visitor

for Lee

$\mathcal{T}$alk about mean! Odd Henderson was the meanest human creature in my experience.

And I'm speaking of a twelve-year-old boy, not some grownup who has had the time to ripen a naturally evil disposition. At least, Odd was twelve in 1932, when we were both second-graders attending a small-town school in rural Alabama.

Tall for his age, a bony boy with muddy-red hair and narrow yellow eyes, he towered over all his classmates—would have in any event, for the rest of us were only seven or eight years old. Odd had failed first grade twice and was now serving his second term in the second grade. This sorry record wasn't due to dumbness—Odd was intelligent, maybe cunning is a better word—but he took after the rest of the Hendersons. The whole family (there were ten of them, not counting Dad Henderson, who was a bootlegger and usually in jail, all scrunched together in a four-room house next door to a Negro church) was a shiftless, surly bunch, every one of them ready to do you a bad turn; Odd wasn't the worst of the lot, and brother, that is *saying* something.

Many children in our school came from families poorer than the Hendersons; Odd had a pair of shoes, while some boys, girls too, were forced to go barefoot right through the bitterest weather—that's how hard the Depression had hit Alabama. But nobody, I don't care who, looked as down-and-out as Odd—a skinny, freckled scarecrow in sweaty cast-off overalls that would have been a humiliation to a chain-gang convict. You might have felt pity for him if he hadn't been so hateful. All the kids feared him, not just us younger kids, but even boys his own age and older.

Nobody ever picked a fight with him except one time a girl named Ann "Jumbo" Finchburg, who happened to be the other town bully. Jumbo, a sawed-off but solid tomboy with an all-hell-let-loose wrestling technique, jumped Odd from behind during recess one dull morning, and it took three teachers, each of whom must have wished the combatants would kill each other, a good long while to separate them. The result was a sort of draw: Jumbo lost a tooth and half her hair and developed a grayish cloud in her left eye (she never could see clear again); Odd's afflictions included a broken thumb, plus scratch scars that will stay with him to the day they shut his coffin. For months afterward, Odd played every kind of trick to goad Jumbo into a rematch; but Jumbo had gotten her licks and gave him considerable berth. As I would have done if he'd let me; alas, I was the object of Odd's relentless attentions.

Considering the era and locale, I was fairly well

off—living, as I did, in a high-ceilinged old country house situated where the town ended and the farms and forests began. The house belonged to distant relatives, elderly cousins, and these cousins, three maiden ladies and their bachelor brother, had taken me under their roof because of a disturbance among my more immediate family, a custody battle that, for involved reasons, had left me stranded in this somewhat eccentric Alabama household. Not that I was unhappy there; indeed, moments of those few years turned out to be the happiest part of an otherwise difficult childhood, mainly because the youngest of the cousins, a woman in her sixties, became my first friend. As she was a child herself (many people thought her less than that, and murmured about her as though she were the twin of poor nice Lester Tucker, who roamed the streets in a sweet daze), she understood children, and understood me absolutely.

Perhaps it was strange for a young boy to have as his best friend an aging spinster, but neither of us had an ordinary outlook or background, and so it was inevitable, in our separate loneliness, that we should come to share a friendship apart. Except for the hours I spent at school, the three of us, me and old Queenie, our feisty little rat terrier, and Miss Sook, as everyone called my friend, were almost always together. We hunted herbs in the woods, went fishing on remote creeks (with dried sugarcane stalks for fishing poles) and gathered curious ferns and greeneries that we transplanted and grew with trailing flourish in tin pails and chamber pots. Mostly, though, our life was lived in the kitchen—a farmhouse kitchen, dominated by a big black wood-burning stove, that was often dark and sunny at the same time.

Miss Sook, sensitive as shy-lady fern, a recluse who had never traveled beyond the county boundaries, was totally unlike her brother and sisters, the latter being down-to-earth, vaguely masculine ladies who operated a dry-goods store and several other business ventures. The brother, Uncle B., owned a number of cotton farms scattered around the countryside; because he refused to drive a car or endure any contact whatever with mobilized machinery, he rode horseback, jogging all day from one property to another. He was a kind man, though a silent one: he grunted yes or no, and really never opened his mouth except to feed it. At every meal he had the appetite of an Alaskan grizzly after a winter's hibernation, and it was Miss Sook's task to fill him up.

Breakfast was our principal meal; midday dinner, except on Sundays, and supper were casual menus, often composed of leftovers from the morning. These breakfasts, served promptly at 5:30 A.M., were regular stomach swellers. To the present day I retain a nostalgic hunger for those cockcrow repasts of ham and fried chicken, fried pork chops, fried catfish, fried squirrel (in season), fried eggs, hominy grits with gravy, black-eyed peas, collards with collard liquor and cornbread to mush it in, biscuits, pound cake, pancakes and molasses, honey in the comb, homemade jams and jellies, sweet milk, buttermilk, coffee chicory-flavored and hot as Hades.

The cook, accompanied by her assistants, Queenie

and myself, rose every morning at four to fire the stove and set the table and get everything started. Rising at that hour was not the hardship it may sound; we were used to it, and anyway we always went to bed as soon as the sun dropped and the birds had settled in the trees. Also, my friend was not as frail as she seemed; though she had been sickly as a child and her shoulders were hunched, she had strong hands and sturdy legs. She could move with sprightly, purposeful speed, the frayed tennis shoes she invariably wore squeaking on the waxed kitchen floor, and her distinguished face, with its delicately clumsy features and beautiful, youthful eyes, bespoke a fortitude that suggested it was more the reward of an interior spiritual shine than the visible surface of mere mortal health.

Nevertheless, depending on the season and the number of hands employed on Uncle B.'s farms, there were sometimes as many as fifteen people sitting down to those dawn banquets; the hands were entitled to one hot meal a day—it was part of their wages. Supposedly, a Negro woman came in to help wash the dishes, make the beds, clean the house and do the laundry. She was lazy and unreliable but a lifelong friend of Miss Sook's—which meant that my friend would not consider replacing her and simply did the work herself. She chopped firewood, tended a large menagerie of chickens, turkeys and hogs, scrubbed, dusted, mended all our clothes; yet when I came home from school, she was always eager to keep me company—to play a card game named Rook or rush off on a mushroom hunt or have a pillow fight or, as we sat in the kitchen's waning afternoon light, help me with homework.

She loved to pore over my textbooks, the geography atlas especially ("Oh, Buddy," she would say, because she called me Buddy, "just think of it—a lake named Titicaca. That really exists somewhere in the world"). My education was her education, as well. Due to her childhood illness, she had had almost no schooling; her handwriting was a series of jagged eruptions, the spelling a highly personal and phonetic affair. I could already write and read with a smoother assurance than she was capable of (though she managed to "study" one

The Thanksgiving Visitor

Bible chapter every day, and never missed "Little Or-
phan Annie" or "The Katzenjammer Kids," comics carried by the Mobile paper). She took a bristling pride in
"our" report cards ("Gosh, Buddy! Five A's. Even arith-
metic. I didn't dare to hope we'd get an A in arith-
metic"). It was a mystery to her why I hated school,
why some mornings I wept and pleaded with Uncle B.,
the deciding voice in the house, to let me stay home.

Of course it wasn't that I hated school; what I
hated was Odd Henderson. The torments he con-
trived! For instance, he used to wait for me in the shad-
ows under a water oak that darkened an edge of the
school grounds; in his hand he held a paper sack
stuffed with prickly cockleburs collected on his way to
school. There was no sense in trying to outrun him, for
he was quick as a coiled snake; like a rattler, he struck,
slammed me to the ground and, his slitty eyes gleeful,
rubbed the burrs into my scalp. Usually a circle of kids
ganged around to titter, or pretend to; they didn't really
think it funny; but Odd made them nervous and ready
to please. Later, hiding in a toilet in the boys' room, I

would untangle the burrs knotting my hair; this took forever and always meant missing the first bell.

Our second-grade teacher, Miss Armstrong, was sympathetic, for she suspected what was happening; but eventually, exasperated by my continual tardiness, she raged at me in front of the whole class: "Little mister big britches. What a big head he has! Waltzing in here twenty minutes after the bell. A half hour." Whereupon I lost control; I pointed at Odd Henderson and shouted: "Yell at him. He's the one to blame. The sonafabitch."

I knew a lot of curse words, yet even I was shocked when I heard what I'd said resounding in an awful silence, and Miss Armstrong, advancing toward me clutching a heavy ruler, said, "Hold out your hands, sir. Palms up, sir." Then, while Odd Henderson watched with a small citric smile, she blistered the palms of my hands with her brass-edged ruler until the room blurred.

It would take a page in small print to list the imaginative punishments Odd inflicted, but what I resented and suffered from most was the sense of dour expectations he induced. Once, when he had me pinned against a wall, I asked him straight out what had I done to make him dislike me so much; suddenly he relaxed, let me loose and said, "You're a sissy. I'm just straightening you out." He was right, I was a sissy of sorts, and the moment he said it, I realized there was nothing I could do to alter his judgment, other than toughen myself to accept and defend the fact.

As soon as I regained the peace of the warm kitchen, where Queenie might be gnawing an old dug-up bone and my friend puttering with a piecrust, the weight of Odd Henderson would blessedly slide from my shoulders. But too often at night, the narrow lion eyes loomed in my dreams while his high, harsh voice, pronouncing cruel promises, hissed in my ears.

My friend's bedroom was next to mine; occasionally cries arising from my nightmare upheavals wakened her; then she would come and shake me out of an Odd Henderson coma. "Look," she'd say, lighting a lamp, "you've even scared Queenie. She's shaking."

And, "Is it a fever? You're wringing wet. Maybe we ought to call Doctor Stone." But she knew that it wasn't a fever, she knew that it was because of my troubles at school, for I had told and told her how Odd Henderson treated me.

But now I'd stopped talking about it, never mentioned it any more, because she refused to acknowledge that any human could be as bad as I made him out. Innocence, preserved by the absence of experience that had always isolated Miss Sook, left her incapable of encompassing an evil so complete.

"Oh," she might say, rubbing heat into my chilled hands, "he only picks on you out of jealousy. He's not smart and pretty as you are." Or, less jestingly, "The thing to keep in mind, Buddy, is this boy can't help acting ugly; he doesn't know any different. All those Henderson children have had it hard. And you can lay that at Dad Henderson's door. I don't like to say it, but that man never was anything except a mischief and a fool. Did you know Uncle B. horsewhipped him once? Caught him beating a dog and horsewhipped him on the spot. The best thing that ever happened was when they locked him up at State Farm. But I remember Molly Henderson before she married Dad. Just fifteen or sixteen she was, and fresh from somewhere across the river. She worked for Sade Danvers down the road, learning to be a dressmaker. She used to pass here and see me hoeing in the garden—such a polite girl, with lovely red hair, and so appreciative of everything; sometimes I'd give her a bunch of sweet peas or a japonica, and she was always so appreciative. Then she began strolling by arm in arm with Dad Henderson—and him so much older and a perfect rascal, drunk or sober. Well, the Lord must have His reasons. But it's a shame; Molly can't be more than thirty-five, and there she is without a tooth in her head or a dime to her name. Nothing but a houseful of children to feed. You've got to take all that into account, Buddy, and be patient."

Patient! What was the use of discussing it? Finally, though, my friend did comprehend the seriousness of my despair. The realization arrived in a quiet way and was not the outcome of unhappy midnight wakings or pleading scenes with Uncle B. It happened one rainy November twilight when we were sitting alone in the kitchen close by the dying stove fire; supper was over, the dishes stacked, and Queenie was tucked in a rocker, snoring. I could hear my friend's whispery voice weaving under the skipping noise of rain on the roof, but my mind was on my worries and I was not attending, though I was aware that her subject was Thanksgiving, then a week away.

My cousins had never married (Uncle B. had *almost* married, but his fiancée returned the engagement ring when she saw that sharing a house with three very individual spinsters would be part of the bargain); however, they boasted extensive family connections throughout the vicinity: cousins aplenty, and an aunt, Mrs. Mary Taylor Wheelwright, who was one hundred and three years old. As our house was the largest and the most conveniently located, it was traditional for these relations to aim themselves our way every year at Thanksgiving; though there were seldom fewer than thirty celebrants, it was not an onerous chore, because we provided only the setting and an ample number of stuffed turkeys.

The guests supplied the trimmings, each of them contributing her particular specialty: a cousin twice removed, Harriet Parker from Flomaton, made perfect ambrosia, transparent orange slices combined with freshly ground coconut; Harriet's sister Alice usually arrived carrying a dish of whipped sweet potatoes and raisins; the Conklin tribe, Mr. and Mrs. Bill Conklin and their quartet of handsome daughters, always brought a delicious array of vegetables canned during the summer. My own favorite was a cold banana pudding—a guarded recipe of the ancient aunt who, despite her longevity, was still domestically energetic; to our sorrow she took the secret with her when she died in 1934, age one hundred and five (and it wasn't age that lowered the curtain; she was attacked and trampled by a bull in a pasture).

Miss Sook was ruminating on these matters while

Truman Capote

my mind wandered through a maze as melancholy as
the wet twilight. Suddenly I heard her knuckles rap the
kitchen table: "Buddy!"

"What?"

"You haven't listened to one word."

"Sorry."

"I figure we'll need five turkeys this year. When I
spoke to Uncle B. about it, he said he wanted you to
kill them. Dress them, too."

"But *why*?"

"He says a boy ought to know how to do things like
that."

Slaughtering was Uncle B.'s job. It was an ordeal for
me to watch him butcher a hog or even wring a chicken's
neck. My friend felt the same way; neither of us could
abide any violence bloodier than swatting flies, so I was
taken aback at her casual relaying of this command.

"Well, I won't."

Now she smiled. "Of course you won't. I'll get Bub-
ber or some other colored boy. Pay him a nickel. But,"
she said, her tone descending conspiratorially, "we'll let

72

Uncle B. believe it was you. Then he'll be pleased and stop saying it's such a bad thing."

"What's a bad thing?"

"Our always being together. He says you ought to have other friends, boys your own age. Well, he's right."

"I don't want any other friend."

"Hush, Buddy. Now hush. You've been real good to me. I don't know what I'd do without you. Just become an old crab. But I want to see you happy, Buddy. Strong, able to go out in the world. And you're never going to until you come to terms with people like Odd Henderson and turn them into friends."

"Him! He's the last friend in the world I want."

"Please, Buddy—invite that boy here for Thanksgiving dinner."

Though the pair of us occasionally quibbled, we never quarreled. At first I was unable to believe she meant her request as something more than a sample of poor-taste humor; but then, seeing that she was serious, I realized, with bewilderment, that we were edging toward a falling-out.

73

"I thought you were my *friend*."

"I am, Buddy. Truly."

"If you were, you couldn't think up a thing like that. Odd Henderson hates me. He's my *enemy*."

"He can't hate you. He doesn't know you."

"Well, I hate him."

"Because you don't know him. That's all I ask. The chance for you to know each other a little. Then I think this trouble will stop. And maybe you're right, Buddy, maybe you boys won't ever be friends. But I doubt that he'd pick on you any more."

"You don't understand. You've never hated anybody."

"No, I never have. We're allotted just so much time on earth, and I wouldn't want the Lord to see me wasting mine in any such manner."

"I won't do it. He'd think I was crazy. And I would be."

The rain had let up, leaving a silence that lengthened miserably. My friend's clear eyes contemplated me as though I were a Rook card she was deciding how

74

to play; she maneuvered a salt-pepper lock of hair off her forehead and sighed. "Then *I* will. Tomorrow," she said, "I'll put on my hat and pay a call on Molly Henderson." This statement certified her determination, for I'd never known Miss Sook to plan a call on anyone, not only because she was entirely without social talent, but also because she was too modest to presume a welcome. "I don't suppose there will be much Thanksgiving in their house. Probably Molly would be very pleased to have Odd sit down with us. Oh, I know Uncle B. would never permit it, but the nice thing to do is invite them all."

*M*y laughter woke Queenie; and after a surprised instant, my friend laughed too. Her cheeks pinked and a light flared in her eyes; rising, she hugged me and said, "Oh, Buddy, I knew you'd forgive me and recognize there was some sense to my notion."

She was mistaken. My merriment had other origins. Two. One was the picture of Uncle B. carving turkey for all those cantankerous Hendersons. The second was: It had occurred to me that I had no cause for alarm; Miss Sook might extend the invitation and Odd's mother might accept it in his behalf; but Odd wouldn't show up in a million years.

He would be too proud. For instance, throughout the Depression years, our school distributed free milk and sandwiches to all children whose families were too poor to provide them with a lunch box. But Odd, emaciated as he was, refused to have anything to do with these handouts; he'd wander off by himself and devour a pocketful of peanuts or gnaw a large raw turnip. This kind of pride was characteristic of the Henderson breed: they might steal, gouge the gold out of a dead man's teeth, but they would never accept a gift offered openly, for anything smacking of charity was offensive to them. Odd was sure to figure Miss Sook's invitation as a charitable gesture; or see it—and not incorrectly—as a blackmailing stunt meant to make him ease up on me.

I went to bed that night with a light heart, for I was

certain my Thanksgiving would not be marred by the presence of such an unsuitable visitor.

The next morning I had a bad cold, which was pleasant; it meant no school. It also meant I could have a fire in my room and cream-of-tomato soup and hours alone with Mr. Micawber and David Copperfield: the happiest of stayabeds. It was drizzling again; but true to her promise, my friend fetched her hat, a straw cartwheel decorated with weather-faded velvet roses, and set out for the Henderson home. "I won't be but a minute," she said. In fact, she was gone the better part of two hours. I couldn't imagine Miss Sook sustaining so long a conversation except with me or herself (she talked to herself often, a habit of sane persons of a solitary nature); and when she returned, she did seem drained.

Still wearing her hat and an old loose raincoat, she slipped a thermometer in my mouth, then sat at the foot of the bed. "I like her," she said firmly. "I always have liked Molly Henderson. She does all she can, and the house was clean as Bob Spencer's fingernails"—

Bob Spencer being a Baptist minister famed for his hygienic gleam—"but bitter cold. With a tin roof and the wind right in the room and not a scrap of fire in the fireplace. She offered me refreshment, and I surely would have welcomed a cup of coffee, but I said no. Because I don't expect there was any coffee on the premises. Or sugar.

"It made me feel ashamed, Buddy. It hurts me all the way down to see somebody struggling like Molly. Never able to see a clear day. I don't say people should have everything they want. Though, come to think of it, I don't see what's wrong with that, either. You ought to have a bike to ride, and why shouldn't Queenie have a beef bone every day? Yes, now it's come to me, now I understand: We really all of us ought to have everything we want. I'll bet you a dime that's what the Lord intends. And when all around us we see people who can't satisfy the plainest needs, I feel ashamed. Oh, not of myself, because who am I, an old nobody who never owned a mite; if I hadn't had a family to pay my way, I'd have starved or been sent to the County Home. The shame I feel is for all of us who have anything extra when other people have nothing.

"I mentioned to Molly how we had more quilts here than we could ever use—there's a trunk of scrap quilts in the attic, the ones I made when I was a girl and couldn't go outdoors much. But she cut me off, said the Hendersons were doing just fine, thank you, and the only thing they wanted was Dad to be set free and sent home to his people. 'Miss Sook,' she told me, 'Dad is a good husband, no matter what else he might be.' Meanwhile, she has her children to care for.

"And, Buddy, you must be wrong about her boy Odd. At least partially. Molly says he's a great help to her and a great comfort. Never complains, regardless of how many chores she gives him. Says he can sing good as you hear on the radio, and when the younger children start raising a ruckus, he can quiet them down by singing to them. Bless us," she lamented, retrieving the thermometer, "all we can do for people like Molly is respect them and remember them in our prayers."

The thermometer had kept me silent; now I demanded, "But what about the invitation?"

"Sometimes," she said, scowling at the scarlet thread in the glass, "I think these eyes are giving out. At my age, a body starts to look around very closely. So you'll remember how cobwebs really looked. But to answer your question, Molly was happy to hear you thought enough of Odd to ask him over for Thanksgiving. And," she continued, ignoring my groan, "she said she was sure he'd be tickled to come. Your temperature is just over the hundred mark. I guess you can count on staying home tomorrow. That ought to bring smiles! Let's see you smile, Buddy."

As it happened, I was smiling a good deal during the next few days prior to the big feast, for my cold had advanced to croup and I was out of school the entire period. I had no contact with Odd Henderson and therefore could not personally ascertain his reaction to the invitation; but I imagined it must have made him laugh first and spit next. The prospect of his actually appearing didn't worry me; it was as farfetched a possibility as Queenie snarling at me or Miss Sook betraying my trust in her.

Yet Odd remained a presence, a redheaded silhouette on the threshold of my cheerfulness. Still, I was tantalized by the description his mother had provided; I wondered if it was true he had another side, that somewhere underneath the evil a speck of humaneness existed. But that was impossible! Anybody who believed so would leave their house unlocked when the gypsies came to town. All you had to do was look at him.

Miss Sook was aware that my croup was not as severe as I pretended, and so in the mornings, when the others had absented themselves—Uncle B. to his farms and the sisters to their dry-goods store—she tolerated my getting out of bed and even let me assist in the springlike housecleaning that always preceded the Thanksgiving assembly. There was such a lot to do, enough for a dozen hands. We polished the parlor furniture, the piano, the black curio cabinet (which con-

tained only a fragment of Stone Mountain the sisters
had brought back from a business trip to Atlanta), the
formal walnut rockers and florid Biedermeier pieces—
rubbed them with lemon-scented wax until the place
was shiny as lemon skin and smelled like a citrus grove.
Curtains were laundered and rehung, pillows punched,
rugs beaten; wherever one glanced, dust motes and tiny
feathers drifted in the sparkling November light sifting
through the tall rooms. Poor Queenie was relegated to
the kitchen, for fear she might leave a stray hair, perhaps a flea, in the more dignified areas of the house.

The most delicate task was preparing the napkins
and tablecloths that would decorate the dining room.
The linen had belonged to my friend's mother, who had
received it as a wedding gift; though it had been used
only once or twice a year, say two hundred times in the
past eighty years, nevertheless it was eighty years old,
and mended patches and freckled discolorations were
apparent. Probably it had not been a fine material to
begin with, but Miss Sook treated it as though it had
been woven by golden hands on heavenly looms: "My

mother said, 'The day may come when all we can offer is well water and cold cornbread, but at least we'll be able to serve it on a table set with proper linen.'"

At night, after the day's dashing about and when the rest of the house was dark, one feeble lamp burned late while my friend, propped in bed with napkins massed on her lap, repaired blemishes and tears with thread and needle, her forehead crumpled, her eyes cruelly squeezed, yet illuminated by the fatigued rapture of a pilgrim approaching an altar at journey's end.

From hour to hour, as the shivery tolls of the faraway courthouse clock numbered ten and eleven and twelve, I would wake up and see her lamp still lit, and would drowsily lurch into her room to reprimand her: "You ought to be asleep!"

"In a minute, Buddy. I can't just now. When I think of all the company coming, it scares me. Starts my head whirling," she said, ceasing to stitch and rubbing her eyes. "Whirling with stars."

Chrysanthemums: some as big as a baby's head.

Bundles of curled penny-colored leaves with flickering lavender underhues. "Chrysanthemums," my friend commented as we moved through our garden stalking flower-show blossoms with decapitating shears, "are like lions. Kingly characters. I always expect them to *spring*. To turn on me with a growl and a roar."

It was the kind of remark that caused people to wonder about Miss Sook, though I understand that only in retrospect, for I always knew just what she meant, and in this instance the whole idea of it, the notion of lugging all those growling gorgeous roaring lions into the house and caging them in tacky vases (our final decorative act on Thanksgiving Eve) made us so giggly and giddy and stupid we were soon out of breath.

"Look at Queenie," my friend said, stuttering with mirth. "Look at her ears, Buddy. Standing straight up. She's thinking, Well, what kind of lunatics are these I'm mixed up with? Ah, Queenie. Come here, honey. I'm going to give you a biscuit dipped in hot coffee."

A lively day, that Thanksgiving. Lively with on-and-off showers and abrupt sky clearings accompanied by thrusts of raw sun and sudden bandit winds snatching autumn's leftover leaves.

The noises of the house were lovely, too: pots and pans and Uncle B.'s unused and rusty voice as he stood in the hall in his creaking Sunday suit, greeting our guests as they arrived. A few came by horseback or mule-drawn wagon, the majority in shined-up farm trucks and rackety flivvers. Mr. and Mrs. Conklin and their four beautiful daughters drove up in a mint-green 1932 Chevrolet (Mr. Conklin was well off; he owned several fishing smackers that operated out of Mobile), an object which aroused warm curiosity among the men present; they studied and poked it and all but took it apart.

The first guests to arrive were Mrs. Mary Taylor Wheelwright, escorted by her custodians, a grandson and his wife. She was a pretty little thing, Mrs. Wheelwright; she wore her age as lightly as the tiny red bonnet that, like the cherry on a vanilla sundae, sat perkily atop her milky hair. "Darlin' Bobby," she said, hugging Uncle B., "I realize we're an itty-bit early, but you know me, always punctual to a fault." Which was an apology deserved, for it was not yet nine o'clock and guests weren't expected much before noon.

However, *everybody* arrived earlier than we intended—except the Perk McCloud family, who suffered two blowouts in the space of thirty miles and arrived in such a stomping temper, particularly Mr. McCloud, that we feared for the china. Most of these people lived year-round in lonesome places hard to get away from: isolated farms, whistle-stops and crossroads, empty river hamlets or lumber-camp communities deep in the pine forests; so of course it was eagerness that caused them to be early, primed for an affectionate and memorable gathering.

*A*nd so it was. Some while ago, I had a letter from one of the Conklin sisters, now the wife of a naval captain and living in San Diego; she wrote: "I think of you often around this time of year, I suppose because of what happened at one of our Alabama Thanksgivings.

It was a few years before Miss Sook died—would it be 1933? Golly, I'll never forget that day."

By noon, not another soul could be accommodated in the parlor, a hive humming with women's tattle and womanly aromas: Mrs. Wheelwright smelled of lilac water and Annabel Conklin like geraniums after rain. The odor of tobacco fanned out across the porch, where most of the men had clustered, despite the wavering weather, the alternations between sprinkles of rain and sunlit wind squalls. Tobacco was a substance alien to the setting; true, Miss Sook now and again secretly dipped snuff, a taste acquired under unknown tutelage and one she refused to discuss; her sisters would have been mortified had they suspected, and Uncle B., too, for he took a harsh stand on all stimulants, condemning them morally and medically.

The virile redolence of cigars, the pungent nip of pipe smoke, the tortoiseshell richness they evoked, constantly lured me out of the parlor onto the porch, though it was the parlor I preferred, due to the presence of the Conklin sisters, who played by turn our untuned piano with a gifted, rollicking lack of airs. "In-dian Love Call" was among their repertoire, and also a 1918 war ballad, the lament of a child pleading with a house thief, entitled "Don't Steal Daddy's Medals, He Won Them for Bravery." Annabel played and sang it; she was the oldest of the sisters and the loveliest, though it was a chore to pick among them, for they were like quadruplets of unequal height. One thought of apples, compact and flavorful, sweet but cider-tart; their hair, loosely plaited, had the blue luster of a well-groomed ebony racehorse, and certain features, eye-brows, noses, lips when smiling, tilted in an original style that added humor to their charms. The nicest thing was that they were a bit plump: "pleasingly plump" describes it precisely.

It was while listening to Annabel at the piano, and falling in love with her, that I felt Odd Henderson. I say *felt* because I was aware of him before I saw him: the sense of peril that warns, say, an experienced woods-man of an impending encounter with a rattler or bob-cat alerted me.

I turned, and there the fellow stood at the parlor entrance, half in, half out. To others he must have seemed simply a grubby twelve-year-old beanpole who had made some attempt to rise to the event by parting and slicking his difficult hair, the comb grooves were still damply intact. But to me he was as unexpected and sinister as a genie released from a bottle. What a dumbhead I'd been to think he wouldn't show up! Only a dunce wouldn't have guessed that he would come out of spite: the joy of spoiling for me this awaited day.

However, Odd had not yet seen me: Annabel, her firm, acrobatic fingers somersaulting over the warped piano keys, had diverted him, for he was watching her, lips separated, eyes slitted, as though he had come upon her disrobed and cooling herself in the local river. It was as if he were contemplating some wished-for vision; his already red ears had become pimiento. The entrancing scene so dazed him I was able to squeeze directly past him and run along the hall to the kitchen. "He's here!"

My friend had completed her work hours earlier;

moreover she had two colored women helping out. Nevertheless she had been hiding in the kitchen since our party started, under a pretense of keeping the exiled Queenie company. In truth, she was afraid of mingling with any group, even one composed of relatives, which was why, despite her reliance on the Bible and its Hero, she rarely went to church. Although she loved all children and was at ease with them, she was not acceptable as a child, yet she could not accept herself as a peer of grownups and in a collection of them behaved like an awkward young lady, silent and rather astonished. But the *idea* of parties exhilarated her; what a pity she couldn't take part invisibly, for then how festive she would have felt.

I noticed that my friend's hands were trembling; so were mine. Her usual outfit consisted of calico dresses, tennis shoes and Uncle B.'s discarded sweaters; she had no clothes appropriate to starchy occasions. Today she was lost inside something borrowed from one of her stout sisters, a creepy navy-blue dress its owner

had worn to every funeral in the county since time remembered.

"He's here," I informed her for the third time. "Odd
Henderson."

"Then why aren't you with him?" she said admon-
ishingly. "That's not polite, Buddy. He's your particular
guest. You ought to be out there seeing he meets everybody and has a good time."

"I *can't*. I can't speak to him."

Queenie was curled on her lap, having a head rub;
my friend stood up, dumping Queenie and disclosing a
stretch of navy-blue material sprinkled with dog hair,
said *"Buddy*. You mean you haven't spoken to that boy!"
My rudeness obliterated her timidity; taking me by the
hand, she steered me to the parlor.

She need not have fretted over Odd's welfare. The
charms of Annabel Conklin had drawn him to the
piano. Indeed, he was scrunched up beside her on
the piano seat, sitting there studying her delightful
profile, his eyes opaque as the orbs of the stuffed whale

I'd seen that summer when a touring honky-tonk passed through town (it was advertised as *The Original Moby Dick,* and it cost five cents to view the remains—what a bunch of crooks!). As for Annabel, she would flirt with anything that walked or crawled—no, that's unfair, for it was really a form of generosity, of simply being alive. Still, it gave me a hurt to see her playing cute with that mule skinner.

Hauling me onward, my friend introduced herself to him: "Buddy and I, we're so happy you could come." Odd had the manners of a billy goat: he didn't stand up or offer his hand, hardly looked at her and at me not at all. Daunted but dead game, my friend said: "Maybe Odd will sing us a tune. I know he can; his mother told me so. Annabel, sugar, play something Odd can sing."

Reading back, I see that I haven't thoroughly described Odd Henderson's ears—a major omission, for they were a pair of eye-catchers, like Alfalfa's in the *Our Gang* comedy pictures. Now, because of Annabel's flattering receptivity to my friend's request, his ears became so beet-bright it made your eyes smart. He mumbled, he shook his head hangdog; but Annabel said: "Do you know 'I Have Seen the Light'?" He didn't, but her next suggestion was greeted with a grin of recognition; the biggest fool could tell his modesty was all put on.

Giggling, Annabel struck a rich chord, and Odd, in a voice precociously manly, sang: "When the red, red robin comes bob, bob, bobbin' along." The Adam's apple in his tense throat jumped; Annabel's enthusiasm accelerated; the women's shrill hen chatter slackened as they became aware of the entertainment. Odd was good, he could sing for sure, and the jealousy charging through me had enough power to electrocute a murderer. Murder was what I had in mind; I could have killed him as easily as swat a mosquito. Easier.

Once more, unnoticed even by my friend, who was absorbed in the musicale, I escaped the parlor and sought The Island. That was the name I had given a place in the house where I went when I felt blue or inexplicably exuberant or just when I wanted to think things over. It was a mammoth closet attached to our only bathroom; the bathroom itself, except for its sanitary fixtures, was like a cozy winter parlor, with a horsehair love seat, scatter rugs, a bureau, a fireplace and framed reproductions of "The Doctor's Visit," "September Morn," "The Swan Pool" and calendars galore.

There were two small stained-glass windows in the closet; lozenge-like patterns of rose, amber and green light filtered through the windows, which looked out on the bathroom proper. Here and there patches of color had faded from the glass or been chipped away; by applying an eye to one of these clearings, it was possible to identify the room's visitors. After I'd been secluded there awhile, brooding over my enemy's success, footsteps intruded: Mrs. Mary Taylor Wheelwright, who stopped before a mirror, smacked her face with a powder puff, rouged her antique cheeks and then, perusing the effect, announced: "Very nice, Mary. Even if Mary says so herself."

It is well known that women outlive men; could it merely be superior vanity that keeps them going? Anyway, Mrs. Wheelwright sweetened my mood, so when, following her departure, a heartily rung dinner bell sounded through the house, I decided to quit my refuge and enjoy the feast, regardless of Odd Henderson.

But just then footsteps echoed again. *He* appeared, looking less sullen than I'd ever seen him. Strutty. Whistling. Unbuttoning his trousers and letting go with a forceful splash, he whistled along, jaunty as a jaybird in a field of sunflowers. As he was leaving, an open box on the bureau summoned his attention. It was a cigar box in which my friend kept recipes torn out of newspapers and other junk, as well as a cameo brooch her father had long ago given her. Sentimental value aside, her imagination had conferred upon the object a rare costliness; whenever we had cause for serious grievance against her sisters or Uncle B., she would say, "Never mind, Buddy. We'll sell my cameo and go away. We'll take the bus to New Orleans." Though never discussing what we would do once we arrived in New Orleans, or what we would live on after the cameo money ran out, we both relished this fantasy. Perhaps each of us secretly realized the brooch was only a Sears Roebuck novelty; all the same, it seemed to us a talisman of true, though untested, magic: a charm that promised us our freedom if indeed we did decide to pursue our luck in fabled spheres. So my friend never wore it, for it was too much a treasure to risk its loss or damage.

Now I saw Odd's sacrilegious fingers reach toward it, watched him bounce it in the palm of his hand, drop it back in the box and turn to go. Then return. This time he swiftly retrieved the cameo and sneaked it into his pocket. My boiling first instinct was to rush out of the closet and challenge him; at that moment, I believe I could have pinned Odd to the floor. *But*— Well, do you recall how, in simpler days, funny-paper artists used to illustrate the birth of an idea by sketching an incandescent light bulb above the brow of Mutt or Jeff or whomever? That's how it was with me: a sizzling light bulb suddenly radiated my brain. The shock and brilliance of it made me burn and shiver—laugh, too.

Odd had handed me an ideal instrument for revenge, one that would make up for all the cockleburs.

In the dining room, long tables had been joined to shape a T. Uncle B. was at the upper center, Mrs. Mary Taylor Wheelwright at his right and Mrs. Conklin at his left. Odd was seated between two of the Conklin sisters, one of them Annabel, whose compliments kept him in top condition. My friend had put herself at the foot of the table among the youngest children; according to her, she had chosen the position because it provided quicker access to the kitchen, but of course it was because that was where she wished to be. Queenie, who had somehow got loose, was under the table—trembling and wagging with ecstasy as she skittered between the rows of legs—but nobody seemed to object, probably because they were hypnotized by the uncarved, lusciously glazed turkeys and the excellent aromas rising from dishes of okra and corn, onion fritters and hot mince pies.

My own mouth would have watered if it hadn't gone bone-dry at the heart-pounding prospect of total revenge. For a second, glancing at Odd Henderson's suffused face, I experienced a fragmentary regret, but I really had no qualms.

Uncle B. recited grace. Head bowed, eyes shut, calloused hands prayerfully placed, he intoned: "Bless You, O Lord, for the bounty of our table, the varied fruits we can be thankful for on this Thanksgiving Day of a troubled year"—his voice, so infrequently heard, croaked with the hollow imperfections of an old organ in an abandoned church—"Amen."

Then, as chairs were adjusted and napkins rustled, the necessary pause I'd been listening for arrived. "Someone here is a thief." I spoke clearly and repeated the accusation in even more measured tones: "Odd Henderson is a thief. He stole Miss Sook's cameo."

Napkins gleamed in suspended, immobilized hands. Men coughed, the Conklin sisters gasped in quadruplet unison and little Perk McCloud, Jr., began to hiccup, as very young children will when startled.

My friend, in a voice teetering between reproach and anguish, said, "Buddy doesn't mean that. He's only teasing."

"I do mean it. If you don't believe me, go look in your box. The cameo isn't there. Odd Henderson has it in his pocket."

"Buddy's had a bad croup," she murmured. "Don't blame him, Odd. He hasn't a notion what he's saying."

I said, "Go look in your box. I saw him take it."

Uncle B., staring at me with an alarming wintriness, took charge. "Maybe you'd better," he told Miss Sook. "That should settle the matter."

It was not often that my friend disobeyed her brother; she did not now. But her pallor, the mortified angle of her shoulders, revealed with what distaste she accepted the errand. She was gone only a minute, but her absence seemed an eon. Hostility sprouted and surged around the table like a thorn-encrusted vine growing with uncanny speed—and the victim trapped in its tendrils was not the accused, but his accuser.

Stomach sickness gripped me; Odd, on the other hand, seemed calm as a corpse.

Miss Sook returned, smiling. "Shame on you, Buddy," she chided, shaking a finger. "Playing that kind of joke. My cameo was exactly where I left it."

Uncle B. said, "Buddy, I want to hear you apologize to our guest."

"No, he don't have to do that," Odd Henderson said, rising. "He was telling the truth." He dug into his pocket and put the cameo on the table. "I wish I had some excuse to give. But I ain't got none." Starting for the door, he said, "You must be a special lady, Miss Sook, to fib for me like that." And then, damn his soul, he walked right out of there.

So did I. Except I ran. I pushed back my chair, knocking it over. The crash triggered Queenie; she scooted from under the table, barked and bared her teeth. And Miss Sook, as I went past her, tried to stop me: "Buddy!" But I wanted no part of her *or* Queenie. That dog had snarled at me and my friend had taken Odd Henderson's side, she'd lied to save his skin, betrayed our friendship, my love: things I'd thought could never happen.

Simpson's pasture lay below the house, a meadow brilliant with high November gold and russet grass. At the edge of the pasture there were a gray barn, a pig corral, a fenced-in chicken yard and a smokehouse. It was the smokehouse I slipped into, a black chamber cool on even the hottest summer days. It had a dirt floor and a smoke pit that smelled of hickory cinders and creosote; rows of hams hung from rafters. It was a place I'd always been wary of, but now its darkness seemed sheltering. I fell on the ground, my ribs heaving like the gills of a beach-stranded fish; and I didn't care that I was demolishing my one nice suit, the one with long trousers, by thrashing about on the floor in a messy mixture of earth and ashes and pork grease.

One thing I knew: I was going to quit that house, that town, that night. Hit the road. Hop a freight and head for California. Make my living shining shoes in Hollywood. Fred Astaire's shoes. Clark Gable's. Or—

maybe I just might become a movie star myself. Look at Jackie Cooper. Oh, they'd be sorry then. When I was rich and famous and refused to answer their letters and even telegrams, probably.

Suddenly I thought of something that would make them even sorrier. The door to the shed was ajar, and a knife of sunshine exposed a shelf supporting several bottles. Dusty bottles with skull-and-crossbone labels. If I drank from one of those, then all of them up there in the dining room, the whole swilling and gobbling caboodle, would know what sorry was. It was worth it, if only to witness Uncle B.'s remorse when they found me cold and stiff on the smokehouse floor; worth it to hear the human wails and Queenie's howls as my coffin was lowered into cemetery depths.

The only hitch was, I wouldn't actually be able to see or hear any of this: how could I, being dead? And unless one can observe the guilt and regret of the mourners, surely there is nothing satisfactory about being dead?

Uncle B. must have forbidden Miss Sook to go

look for me until the last guest had left the table. It was late afternoon before I heard her voice floating across the pasture; she called my name softly, forlornly as a mourning dove. I stayed where I was and did not answer.

It was Queenie who found me; she came sniffing around the smokehouse and yapped when she caught my scent, then entered and crawled toward me and licked my hand, an ear and a cheek; she knew she had treated me badly.

Presently, the door swung open and the light widened. My friend said, "Come here, Buddy." And I wanted to go to her. When she saw me, she laughed. "Goodness, boy. You look dipped in tar and all ready for feathering." But there were no recriminations or references to my ruined suit.

Queenie trotted off to pester some cows; and trailing after her into the pasture, we sat down on a tree stump. "I saved you a drumstick," she said, handing me a parcel wrapped in waxed paper. "And your favorite piece of turkey. The pulley."

The hunger that direr sensations had numbed now hit me like a belly-punch. I gnawed the drumstick clean, then stripped the pulley, the sweet part of the turkey around the wishbone.

While I was eating, Miss Sook put her arm around my shoulders. "There's just this I want to say, Buddy. Two wrongs never made a right. It was wrong of him to take the cameo. But we don't know why he took it. Maybe he never meant to keep it. Whatever his reason, it can't have been calculated. Which is why what you did was much worse: you *planned* to humiliate him. It was deliberate. Now listen to me, Buddy: there is only one unpardonable sin—*deliberate cruelty*. All else can be forgiven. That, never. Do you understand me, Buddy?"

I did, dimly, and time has taught me that she was right. But at that moment I mainly comprehended that because my revenge had failed, my method must have been wrong. Odd Henderson had emerged—how? why?—as someone superior to me, even more honest.

"Do you, Buddy? Understand?"

"Sort of. Pull," I said, offering her one prong of the wishbone.

We split it; my half was the larger, which entitled me to a wish. She wanted to know what I'd wished.

"That you're still my friend."

"Dumbhead," she said, and hugged me.

"Forever?"

"I won't be here forever, Buddy. Nor will you." Her voice sank like the sun on the pasture's horizon, was silent a second and then climbed with the strength of a new sun. "But yes, forever. The Lord willing, you'll be here long after I've gone. And as long as you remember me, then we'll always be together." . . .

Afterward, Odd Henderson let me alone. He started tussling with a boy his own age, Squirrel McMillan. And the next year, because of Odd's poor grades and general bad conduct, our school principal wouldn't allow him to attend classes, so he spent the winter working as a hand on a dairy farm. The last time I saw him was shortly before he hitchhiked to Mobile, joined the Merchant Marine and disappeared. It must have been the year before I was packed off to a miserable fate in a military academy, and two years prior to my friend's death. That would make it the autumn of 1934.

Miss Sook had summoned me to the garden; she had transplanted a blossoming chrysanthemum bush into a tin washtub and needed help to haul it up the steps onto the front porch, where it would make a fine display. It was heavier than forty fat pirates, and while we were struggling with it ineffectually, Odd Henderson passed along the road. He paused at the garden gate and then opened it, saying, "Let me do that for you, ma'am." Life on a dairy farm had done him a lot of good; he'd thickened, his arms were sinewy and his red coloring had deepened to a ruddy brown. Airily he lifted the big tub and placed it on the porch.

My friend said, "I'm obliged to you, sir. That was neighborly."

"Nothing," he said, still ignoring me.

Miss Sook snapped the stems of her showiest blooms. "Take these to your mother," she told him, handing him the bouquet. "And give her my love."

"Thank you, ma'am. I will."

"Oh, Odd," she called, after he'd regained the road, "be careful! They're lions, you know." But he was already out of hearing. We watched until he turned a bend at the corner, innocent of the menace he carried, the chrysanthemums that burned, that growled and roared against a greenly lowering dusk.